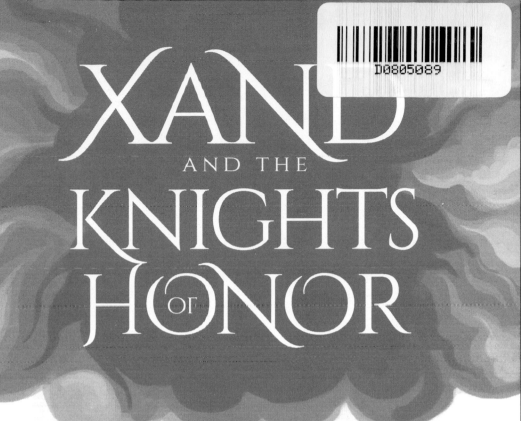

XAND
AND THE
KNIGHTS
HONOR
OF

BOOK ONE OF
THE KNIGHTS OF HONOR SERIES

JAX WARD

Xand and The Knights of Honor
Book One of The Knights of Honor Series

© 2021 Jax Ward

ISBN: 978-1-09836-860-9

CONTENTS

PROLOGUE

The tribe of the Iron Dwarves had been extracting the minerals from the old mines at Run Kazdun Mountain for generations. As long as anyone could remember, the Dwarves were the only suppliers of the iron and copper needed for most items built in their realm. From time to time, other groups would attempt to replace them. This always ended badly. A proud race, the Iron Dwarves ensured their materials were the best in all the land, and that they were the only suppliers. No matter how inexpensive the metals, no one could compete with the quality of their products.

Mining was complex and required care and time from the dwarves to ensure not only the quality of their products but also to ensure every cart sent into the mines returned with the same amount of gold. The Iron Dwarves used the rest of the iron and copper to produce new tools for mining and some of their furniture. However, the dwarves only kept the best of the mined material, as well as all rarities found from time to time, for themselves. These they would sell quietly to the highest bidder, or keep hidden to use for themselves.

One day, such a rarity appeared to a miner named Tordaen, who was concentrating intently on his daily work when a swing of his axe uncovered something he had never seen before. It was a strange, large, yellow gem that glowed with a faint dark color. Tordaen was impressed by the gem, even if he was unsure of what it might be or how he might use it. He could feel in his bones, however, a sense of magic radiating off it. With great care, he removed it from the rock to observe very carefully. As he turned it around, Tordaen noticed something inside the gem, and peered closer to examine it. Even with his eyes pressed directly to it, he could not make out the object moving within. He started walking back to the front of the cave.

Suddenly, Tordaen felt his knees go weak. But he was so obsessed with the gem he would not let go of it. Something compelled him to keep moving. As he climbed out of the mineshaft, his legs finally gave out, and he fell to the ground with the gem stuck to his hands.

No matter how hard he tried to remove it by shaking his hand and trying to ease his grip, he could not let go of it.

Then, Tordaen heard words whispered inside his head. He looked around but saw nothing that was making any sound. Panicking, he tried standing, but managed to get only to his knees. He could not see anything but the gem, the mysterious contents inside of it spinning around faster and faster. The light grew larger until he could see no more, and then, Tordaen disappeared. Where he had stood, the yellow gem floated lightly in the air before slowly carrying itself on the air into the mineshaft. Stones began slowly forming around it, piece by piece fitting together into the shape of a large gargoyle. The creature lifted a nearby dwarf, who had been standing as still as a statue with his mouth wide open in disbelief and terror, by the dwarf's head, and with a small flick of his massive dark grey stone wrist, launched the terrified dwarf out of the mines and across the open space outside it. The last sound the dwarf heard before landing was a deep, low, building roar echoing out of the cave behind him.

CHAPTER
ONE

X and remembered the confusion most of all. He was two, under his bed, thinking his father's shout to "hide" was just part of a game of hide-and-seek. Xand was not concerned, until he heard his parents speak to each other in a hushed conversation.

As he hid, Xand heard his father say to his mother, "They are coming."

The door rattled and his parents scrambled in an attempt to secure it, running over and shoving boards against the door. But it was no use. Small green and orange creatures, breathing out acid, crashed through into the house. Xand still remembers his mother's terrified shout: "Goblins!"

Immediately, Xand realized this was no game. He peeked out from under his bed, and just as he got the nerve to confront the mischievous goblins, he caught his mother's glance, warning him to remain hidden.

As quickly as the goblins arrived, they escaped with his parents. He knew in that instant that they were dead, and he would never see them again. Crouched down in the small space under his bed, Xand wept quietly while thinking about life without his parents. He remained hidden for what seemed like forever when he heard steps again. Fearing the goblins had returned for him, he made himself small trying to disappear into the floorboards.

Light peered into the small space as someone placed a lamp under the bed. Xand looked up to see an overgrown dwarf, who he would come to know as Jork. Xand noticed Jork's long black beard first, and that it matched his short black hair covering his massive head.

"Come here, kid. You will be alright with me," said Jork, extending his right hand to Xand, who slowly took it and climbed out from under the bed. "Let us go. It is not safe for you to be here all by yourself."

Xand was too scared to speak. One second he is hiding under the bed, thinking it was a game of hide and seek, the next he was walking out of his house with a giant dwarf, knowing his parents were dead.

The two walked out the door, and just as they moved away from the farmhouse, Xand stopped for a minute to look back at his home with sadness. Jork said, "Everything will be alright, son. We'll take care of you."

"Where are my Mom and Dad?" asked Xand, finally breaking the silence.

Jork simply carried Xand in his arms and then sighed, only explaining, "They took them to the castle in the village. They will be fine, but you have to be strong for now and know that I will always be there for you." Xand nodded, but knew that Jork was lying to make him feel better.

Jork took Xand to live with Xand's grandparents on his mother's side. They were farmers who lived in an old house in the village, tending their small nearby farm of animals. They took Xand from time to time to visit his old house, coming back in hopes of reuniting with his parents to live together as a family again. Before he could reclaim his home, though, Xand had to learn to work the land, so as he grew, he learned from his grandparents and others in the village.

Xand thought back on all this on his 13th birthday. In the ensuing years, he had quickly learned how much toil and work was involved in farming and how hard his parents and grandparents had worked. By now, Xand managed the farmland and house. Xand was responsible for the chickens, which was a full time job.

He had grown into a capable young man, his favorite blue leather shirt clinging to his slender frame, his brown pants a touch too small, and a brown sash across his shoulder. His hair had grown in light brown and thick, his hazel eyes going from sad from the memory of his parents to happy about the upcoming celebration.

Once a year, Xand's village celebrated the end of the Great War, which happened on Xand's 2nd birthday. He did not know much about the Great War, because the people in his village, like his grandparents and Jork, always refused to talk about it. "This is for the grown ups," they would say, when he would try to get in conversations about it. Even so, he prepared in anticipation of the event.

Xand walked to the stable where Sparkie, a gift from his uncle Lucious, waited to be saddled. Sparkie's black coat was highlighted by a goldish-white mane. While Xand tried to keep Sparkie company, he remained busy and so tired from work that he did not have much time to spend with the horse and let Sparkie run free and fast. When he could find the time to ride and run with Sparkie, Sparkie appreciated every moment, and Xand knew it.

At this moment, though, Sparkie became excited, sensing they were to about to leave on a trip. Before going into the village, Xand stopped by Jork's house. Jork lived in his large blacksmith's shop, of which he was very proud. Because he was known to sell high-quality goods, Jork's customers came from far away, even the next kingdom over, just to purchase the simplest of items.

When Xand arrived at the blacksmith's shop, Zeg—Jork's son— opened the door. When he had first met him, the day Jork saved him from under the bed, Xand was impressed to learn Zeg was just a one year old baby, even though he was already at least a foot taller than Xand, who was 2 at the time. Zeg grew and eventually measured nearly seven-feet six-inches tall at twelve-years-old. His mop of darkish brown hair sat messy on top of his oversized head. Zeg was never seen without his iron armor, even wearing it to bed. The heavy protection it offered was perfect for the clumsy Zeg, awake or asleep. Jork had crafted Zeg's armor lovingly, and as a last resort, after Zeg had fallen down one too many times the moment Jork took his eyes off him.

"Xand, are you ready for the celebration?" Zeg said as he greeted him. Xand waved at him and dismounted Sparkie. He gave him a hug, which turned into him being lifted and carried around on Zeg's back and into the blacksmith's shop.

"Father, look who has arrived!" Zeg announced, and Jork peeked his head above Zeg's shoulders.

The two interrupted Jork as he worked on a special request for a customer from one of the nearby towns, a new brass bell ordered to celebrate the end of the Great War. He had been in a hurry all week to finish it.

"Hello, Xand," Jork said, pointing at the iron cast that released a cloud of steam. "Mind the mold, it is very hot." He stopped for a minute as he placed the iron down, and asked, "How has your day been? Busy at the farm as usual?"

"There are more chickens by the day I think. I'm getting better every year, but it's very hard work. Will you be coming with us to the celebration?" Xand asked.

Jork shook his head, pointed at the cast for the bell, and explained, "Unfortunately, no—I have to finish this bell and deliver it myself. I would have Zeg do it for me, but I'd like him to have some fun, as kids should!" said Jork, who laughed at the top of his lungs as he waved them off. "Go on now. The celebration isn't going to wait for you!"

As Xand and Zeg rode into the village, they talked about what they might find at the celebration. Once there, though, they were pleasantly surprised to find that the reality was practically all of their predictions combined! Large tables holding food and drinks and musicians played throughout the square. The townspeople were always impressed to see Zeg, even though they were terrified when they saw Zeg eat or drink, fearing he would use up the food supplies for the entire season. That would not be a problem tonight.

Zeg exclaimed, "This is great. I wish we could celebrate like this every day!" He immediately headed in the direction of one of the tables, grabbing a piece of meat that was placed on a large plate. Xand watched him while noticing a dark object flying in the blue sky far above. A large winged creature the size of a human approached the town. Xand thought to himself, how can something that looks like stone fly so fast?

He did not have time to consider the answer, as suddenly, the winged creature landed in the town square, destroying decorations in the plaza and toppling over a statue erected as part of the first celebration after the end of the Great War. The townspeople screamed and shouted. "Gargoyle!" Xand heard someone say. He had only read about gargoyles, and had never seen one in person. This gargoyle had huge wings like a bat, big, pointed ears, a distorted angry face with sharp fangs. His arms and legs had long claws, like an animal. Xand shivered with fear.

One boy dared get close enough to see the wicked creature hovering over one of the tables. The child screamed, "Call the guards! Run!"

Xand ran towards a few of the townspeople to prevent them from getting scooped up by the gargoyle that by now had completely destroyed the statue. Xand grabbed the sword from one of the hands of the statue, which was lying on the ground near him. He slashed at the gargoyle, and to his surprise, his sword cut a wing straight off. He did not know how.

Zeg managed to get a hold of it, but it bucked and swung wildly while trying to escape his grip. To its misfortune, Zeg was far stronger than the creature had initially believed. Xand waved the townspeople back to safety.

As he approached the fight between Zeg and the winged creature, Xand noticed that the other hand from the destroyed statue laying on the ground still held the Grand Diamond Mace of Durkan, a weapon used during the Great War. He picked it up, finding it easier to wield than it should have been based on its size and construction, and shouted at Zeg. "Catch!"

Just as Zeg was about to lose his grip on the gargoyle, he caught the mace and swung hard at the creature. When the mace smashed the gargoyle, it transformed to dust, surrounded by blue flames coming from the mace.

As the gargoyle disappeared in front of their eyes, Xand and Zeg were amazed at what they had just done. The guard arrived just as the gargoyle vanished, and when it was safe, the townsfolk came out from the shadows of the village square.

CHAPTER
TWO

Meanwhile, in the enchanted forest, another young soul was also fighting a gargoyle. She had only heard stories about them, stories from the Great War that ended before she was born. Now Yama, a sun fairy, found herself fighting off a large group of gargoyles trying to invade the Fairy Tree. They had caught her by surprise, but Yama quickly recovered.

Reading about the Great War and how close the Gargoyle King came to successfully conquering the land is why she decided to take the mantle of Defender of the Fairies in the first place. She had trained and worked tirelessly to make sure no fairy would ever be hurt by such an enemy, and that she would be prepared to defend her home the next time darkness fell across the land. She had never used her magic in a real fight before, and she found it exhausting. Even so, she was able to fight off gargoyles. By battle's end her energy had been almost fully depleted, both by her effort and because the sun was starting to set. Sun fairies needed the sun to use magic; it was their Source. Yama, like all sun fairies, had blonde hair and blue eyes that sparkled the brightest in the sun. Yama's dress had a golden colored zig-zag pattern that Yama loved, and her translucent wings fluttered rapidly as she recovered from the battle.

"We will never survive if they attack at night. They are too powerful. If the Gargoyle King has returned, I must alert the elders." said Yama. She returned to the top of the tree, where she was met by a crowd of fairies who celebrated her victory over the gargoyles, and she reassured them their protection was guaranteed. "The sun fairies will defend you by day, and the nature fairies will keep watch through the night," she told them. But in her heart, she knew they would need to do more than just defend their home. She didn't know how it would end, but she knew her next step would take her on a path that would change her life forever.

After reassuring the fairies, she turned to go meet the Elders. But for a moment she paused, looked up at the sun to draw in confidence from its warmth. She took a deep breath, and took flight in the direction of the Elders. They received her with gratitude for her courage in battle, but she noticed the worried looks on their faces. For years, the Elders had prepared, believing and saying, "The Gargoyle King is only resting. Someday, he will return." If the gargoyles had really returned, the fairies had to not only prepare to defend themselves but also to warn their allies before they were caught by surprise as well.

The Elders had reached their decision before Yama's wings stopped flapping. She must go the human town of Zendora, they told Yama, and find the blacksmith named Jork. She must hire him to forge the only weapon that could defeat the Gargoyle King. Yama was surprised. In all her years learning about the Gargoyle King, she had never known such a weapon existed.

"What power does it have? How is it built?" Yama asked, with more questions forming in her head than her mouth could say.

The oldest elder stepped forward. Yama had never heard Ellock speak, only seen her sit quietly as those around her made decisions. "Centuries ago, our ancestors forged a weapon from the volcano of Apothos. It had the power to destroy the heart of the Gargoyle King. After the Great War, it was destroyed so that it could not fall into the wrong hands. But we kept one small piece, and from that, we made fairy dust. This dust, when forged with gold and wielded by someone with goodness in their soul, will be powerful enough to stop the Gargoyle King once again." Yama could barely move, she was so rapt by Ellock's words. She did not notice that Ellock had produced a small bag from beneath her armor. She held it out to Yama.

"Here is the pixie dust that must be used to forge the arrow," Ellock said. "Take it and go. If you do not defeat the Gargoyle King, I fear there may be no one else to stop him."

CHAPTER

THREE

Yama set out at once from the Fairy Tree to Zendora, transforming herself into a woman to avoid suspicion as soon as she left. Once she arrived, she stared in astonishment at how the humans lived. Ever since birth, she had heard many stories about their villages. Now, she was excited to see these places and meet humans outside of the battlefield, taking time to enjoy their food and drink and visit memorials of the Great War. After wandering around for a moment to take Zendora in, a farmer selling harvested crops in town took her to the blacksmith's shop.

Inside the blacksmith's shop, Yama was amazed at the shiny and massive pieces hanging from the walls and ceiling. But at the same time, she felt strangely distant from all the artifacts of war on display. These were very different from the ones at the Fairy Tree. Lacking enchantment, they were strong but....cold.

"How can I help you?" asked Jork. He had never seen the woman, and he knew strangers made trouble. He cleaned his hands with an old piece of cloth and approached her, slightly suspicious of her entry into his shop. "Anything in particular you need?" he asked.

"Yes, I do. Would you be Jork, the blacksmith?" asked Yama, hesitating a few seconds before speaking. Jork nodded slowly. Yama said, "I need a special item. I heard you would be able to make it."

"Depending on what you need, and it might cost you," Jork answered. He pointed at some of the weapons and items in his shop. "Everything you see is a sample of my work. If you need something different, I can still probably do it."

"I need a golden arrow—" said Yama.

"What?!" Jork exclaimed, before recovering. "You must be joking, I can't make -- "

She quickly transformed into a fairy, and then just as quickly, changed back into a human. "I am deadly serious. This is an urgent matter."

"An urgent matter—what would you ever need a golden arrow for?" asked Jork. Yama raised her left hand and waved it around. Her magic produced the image of a gargoyle, which vanished swiftly in thin air. "A gargoyle," he asked. "Did you also get attacked by one?"

"Also? Yama asked. "Who else has been attacked?"

"We had one yesterday. It came into the village during a celebration, but you mean to tell me there is more than one?" asked Jork. Yama nodded and waved her left hand again, producing an image of the attack at the Fairy Tree.

"Many came to us. I fended them off, but I am afraid more will come," answered Yama. Jork sighed at the sight and scratched the back of his head. "And I am afraid that the Gargoyle King has been resurrected."

"Impossible! I cannot make you such a thing. You must go at once, please leave, I am very busy," said Jork. Before he finished his sentence, Yama took one of the pixie dust bags from her backpack and presented it to Jork. "Pixie dust?" he asked, astonished.

"Pixie, fairy, and leprechaun dust—more than enough to pay for your services," answered Yama. Jork's eyes opened wide as he saw the size of the bag containing the most valuable substance he's ever seen, and then agreed to make the arrow quickly.

"I'll have it for you before the end of the day," said Jork, leaving Yama behind the desk.

She reached into her pocket and slowly and carefully placed a small bag on the counter. "You must sprinkle some of this dust on the arrow when it is complete. Promise you will. It is the most important part."

He nodded and stares the small bag, his eyes wide with astonishment.

Yama returned to town to continue her tour of this human city. Before the end of the day, though, she returned to the blacksmith's shop where Jork had just finished making the magical golden arrow she requested.

"As promised," Jork said. Turning to Zeg, he said, "Can you give this woman the golden arrow?" Standing on his toes, Zeg grabbed a piece of cloth hidden on the beams of the roof, handing the piece of cloth to Yama. She carefully opened the cloth and removed the golden arrow from it.

CHAPTER
FOUR

X and walked into Jork's shop and noticed Zeg standing close to a woman Xand had never seen before. Since he knew everyone in the village, and knew everyone they knew, he was surprised.

"Xand, come here," Jork said, motioning toward the young man. Xand walked quickly toward Jork. "I think it's time to give you something that belongs to you."

"Something that belongs to me?" Xand asked. Jork signaled to Zeg, who climbed onto the blacksmith's back and reached up into the ceiling rafters to grab a heavy object. Then, Zeg dug deep down into the ground with a large shovel Jork had made him.

Jork returned to Xand and said, "Before your birth, your father left something in my care for you. He never explained its intended purpose or why I had to hide it —but I think I know why now," said Jork. He extended his hand, motioning toward Yama.

"You knew my father?!!" Xand exclaimed, starting and stopping the dozens of questions that entered his mind and fought for the space to become spoken.

Jork cut him off and said, "Xand, we will have time for questions later. I have feared this day would come for a long time. There is not enough time right now to tell you everything. Please, meet Yama—one of the Sun Fairies, a protector of the Fairies and all living creatures."

"Fairy?" Xand asked, his head spinning, "Aren't they smaller and don't they have wings?"

Yama rapidly took her fairy form and then returned to her human form, proving she was a fairy. Xand took a step backward, surprised by this change. "Wow, you can do that?" he asked.

"I can do that and more, young human. This is part of my magic," answered Yama.

Jork patted Xand on his shoulder and pointed to the back door where Zeg returned with a large red shield, encased in iron around the edges. The dead center of the shield was engraved with a gold helmet.

"Is that the gift?" Xand asked, inspecting the item.

"Yes Xand, your father gave this to me, and now I return it to you—its rightful owner," said Jork. Zeg handed the shield to Jork, and then after bowing to him, he presented it to Xand. "I can no longer keep it with me. Plus, I am sure you'll need it."

"But—" Xand said. He slowly took the shield, noticing that, like the diamond mace he gave Zeg, it was lighter than he had expected. As he put it on his left arm, he noticed strange markings on the border of the shield. "Do you know what these are?" he asked.

"No, I do not. I asked your father the same thing when he gave it to me, but he too did not know," said Jork. Yama pointed at some of the markings and nodded in surprise.

"These are magical markings," she said. "I am not familiar with their purpose, but I have seen similar markings on humans in books about the Great War. This is impressive, though. Did you forge this as well?" Yama asked while pointing to the markings. She turned to face Jork, but he simply shrugged.

"No. As I said, the first time I saw this shield was when his father gave it to me," Jork said, pausing to inspect the shield. "This shield looks like it has seen its fair share of combat, but I'm amazed it's in such great shape."

Xand walked around the room, wearing the shield proudly simply because it belonged to his father. He looked down at the shield to inspect it and then asked, "Why would my father have this shield? Was he a warrior?"

Jork looked at him nervously and said, "Xand, I only know what I've told you--nothing else. He gave me this shield to hide, but I don't know if he ever used it or how he came by it. He only told me that in time it would belong to you," Jork said, looking at the sun while it set. Sighing, Jork said, "Xand, go find Wilder. I think you'll need his help on this adventure."

"Adventure?" asked Xand.

CHAPTER
FIVE

The two arrived in town at night, Xand riding Sparkie and Zeg carrying Yama on his back, for which she was very grateful. She wasn't used to the tremendous amount of walking she had to do as a human, and flying would be harder since the sun had gone down.

In town, they searched for Wilder. Whenever they inquired about Wilder, people sighed or grunted at the sound of his name. No one knew where Wilder lived, and they didn't really want to know. All they knew was that he was dangerous, and he usually turned up at night.

"Why does everyone seem to hate Wilder?" asked Yama. Zeg laughed and Xand smiled at her question, exchanging glances with each other.

"Wilder is a great person. He also happens to be a werewolf," Xand said. Alarmed, Yama shifted back to her fairy form, and then, she remembered where she was and switched back again. "But he has the ability to control his werewolf form," Xand added quickly, seeing Yama's face twist in anger.

"Why are you friends with a werewolf? Do you not know what they have done to all creatures—even humans?" asked Yama. Her voice matched her angry face, and Zeg and Xand were confused at her questions.

"No, I wasn't aware they had done anything to us. Wilder has always been very kind to me and Zeg," Xand said, patting Sparkie on the head as they stopped to ask another townsperson about Wilder. Again, they received no answer regarding Wilder's whereabouts.

"Well, we'll have to wait for him," said Xand. The lamps flickered on while they waited at the plaza. Before they knew it, a figure covered in a cloak waved at them in the distance as it approached.

"Xand, Zeg, why are you here so late? Does Jork need something?" the figure asked, removing the cloak to expose the face of a teenage boy not much older than them. He shook his head clear of the hood. His black hair, darker than night and thick like a mane, shook free. "Can I help?"

"Hello Wilder, how are you?" asked Zeg. Xand got off Sparkie, joining Zeg to hug Wilder.

"I'm fine, as usual. I have to go around the fields to keep an eye out for the guards because they're still too afraid to go out. Do you know the Gargoyles are back?" Wilder asked. He laughed at the thought of the frightened guards and smacked his left knee. "But in all seriousness, why are you here so late?"

"Those gargoyles you mentioned have returned everywhere, not just here," answered Yama. Letting go of Zeg, she slid off his back and approached Wilder saying, "You may not know about this because of your mutt behavior."

"Mutt? Excuse me, but who do you think you are?" asked Wilder. Yama slowly transformed herself into her fairy form to which Wilder grunted and replied, "Oh boy, a fairy has left the tree? It must be worse than I imagined." Wilder looked pale. "There is only one explanation. The Gargoyle King has returned."

CHAPTER

SIX

Back in Run Kazdun, The Gargoyle King sat his newly rebuilt body down heavily on the throne of the Iron Dwarves. He had been slowly recovering his power by absorbing the life force of every dwarf inside the mine. Now seated, he emitted an energy that alerted his followers to his presence, and drawing them to him.

The Dark Pixies felt this and were the first ones to respond to his call. Resembling a dark flock of birds, they reunited with him to help rebuild his grand army, offering their dark pixie dust to him in tribute to his greatness. The pixie dust would be used to create his army of zombies and gargoyles to serve him again just as they had done during the Great War.

To the Gargoyle King's surprise, one of his old Captains, the Illustrious Kazanovus, survived the Great War. He had remained in hiding while assisting the remaining gargoyles in their task of finding and restoring their king. When Kazanovus felt the presence of the King, he hurried to Run Kazdun to offer his expertise in leading the armies just as he had done in the past. The King, seeing his army coming back together, prepared to perform his first attack on the closest town he could find, which he learned was called Zendora.

As Kazanovus gathered the troops again, the Gargoyle King infused him with some of his power so he could lead and fight with the might he used in the past. The King promised to provide him more power if he succeeded in this task, as well as a reward for each human he defeated.

When the Gargoyle King was done with his summoning and spells, he ordered Kazanovus to attack immediately under the veil of the night with the assistance of the Dark Pixies who would transport them as close as possible to the town, taking Zendorans off guard by using the element of surprise.

"Once more, I have returned. Bring forth my message to the humans and their dreadful existence. I will not tolerate them after they have seen us as nothing but slaves. Make sure they never forget my message. Burn their town. Leave only a few survivors, so they may talk about what has happened—*and remember*," said the Gargoyle King, his voice echoing in the enormous caverns of the throne room.

The gargoyles screamed with glee while ghastly banshees floated around, producing shrieks that would deafen the hearing of other creatures. Zombies growled as they waited in a mass while the Dark Pixies flew, escaping from the mountain and heading on the road towards Zendora.

CHAPTER
SEVEN

"That is a big leap. We cannot assume the Gargoyle King has returned just because a couple of minions have attacked a couple places," said Xand. The group was in a serious discussion regarding their next steps in dealing with these gargoyle attacks and what it might mean as they walked back towards Zendora. Xand was skeptical about the Gargoyle King's return, even though he knew that his skepticism might be more like hope that it wasn't true.

"The mutt is right. We need to prepare for it being true," said Yama. She was trying to return to her human form, but found herself incapable of summoning enough energy to do so.

"Oh, you're one of *those* fairies—the sun ones. Excuse me, but I think that you're going to need this mutt's help if you can't do anything at night," said Wilder. Yama looked angrily at him while Wilder smiled back at her, exposing his large canines.

"There is no need for this you two. We need to help Yama first, and then we need to prevent what happened at the celebration from happening in other towns," said Xand.

"What are you talking about?" asked Wilder, slightly confused because this was the first of him hearing about the gargoyle attack at Zendora. Xand and Zeg looked shocked.

"The gargoyle that attacked during the celebration—didn't you hear about it?" asked Zeg.

"No, I hadn't," answered Wilder, taking a moment to reflect but only to be interrupted by the smell of decay. "What is that smell? It's so familiar."

"What smell?" asked Xand. Before anyone answered, a sudden outburst of screams from the direction of the town walls that had just come into sight caught their attention. They saw a horde of darkness in the distance approaching and heard the guards on the other side of the town wall shouting in confusion.

"Come on. We must go. They won't stand a chance on their own!" Xand said.

Wilder removed his cloak completely and transformed himself into a large werewolf, roughly the size of Zeg, but wielding two large swords on his back. Yama and Wilder rushed outside to find a large group of zombies and gargoyles approaching the wall under the cover of darkness. As the two rushed into the battle, they quickly realized they were outnumbered.

Zeg used his strength to grab one of the zombies and throw it against a group approaching them, dropping them like bowling pins. Xand could only watch as his companions fought against the invading hordes without much luck.

In a desperate attempt to aid them, he rushed the pack, raising his shield to protect himself against one of the gargoyles attacking him. Xand braced himself as the gargoyle crashed into him. Instead of getting knocked back, Xand saw a large burst of light explode from his shield, and a wave of rainbow colored energy expanded out from it. It trapped the zombies and, in a pulse of light, disintegrated them. Wilder, Zeg, and Yama yelled and charged at the remaining gargoyles. Xand, shaking his head to clear himself from his momentary stunned disbelief, raised his sword and charged into the fight. His sword cut them down in twos and threes, as fast as they could charge into its swooping arc.

As the team fought the gargoyles, Xand noticed Sparkie becoming restless. All of a sudden, Sparkie became larger and larger until he assumed the shape of a large rhinoceros. Xand stared in awe, and suddenly he remembered the note his Uncle Lucious left him: "Sparkie is more than a horse, be kind to him and treat him like a friend, and he will protect you will all his power." Xand saw the full force of that power, as Sparkie rushed into the pack of gargoyles, causing them to suddenly burst into a blue flame that soon flickered out into blackness.

As the last of gargoyles flew away from the battle back towards their leader, the Illustrious Kazanovus saw how quickly his forces had been repelled and was impressed—even though disappointed—to see the humans fend off his army. He took flight and circled high above, just in time to see Xand's shield draw in the rainbow colored energy and Sparkie transform back into a horse. "The shield. Amazing. I did not get my chance to fight the last human who wielded it. This time will be different," said the Illustrious Kazanovus to himself as he flew away from the last screams of his gargoyle soldiers back towards the Gargoyle King.

The town was safe for the night, but Xand knew it was not the end of the danger. This felt like a test, the Gargoyle King probing his town and to find out how strong the forces that might oppose him really were. Xand knew the Gargoyle King would be able to rebuild his army to the size he needed to overwhelm them, and Xand and his friends would be faced with an even greater test.

Xand put his sword back into its holder and slung his shield over his shoulder. He looked Sparkie in the eye and said, "Someday you will have to tell me who you are and where you came from." Sparkie's eyes twinkled, and his head nodded excitedly as he started to neigh.

But that's a story for another day.

EPILOGUE

A small creek flowed outside Zendora's walls. Birds chirped tentatively, as a nervous energy still lingered for both nature and the four new friends sitting together quietly and gazing out into the forest. It was a few days later for Xand, Wilder, Yama and Zeg, but it felt like only minutes had passed. They had barely been able to speak since the battle the other night, each lost in their own thoughts and each uncertain about whether what they had seen was actually real. Xand spoke up first, breaking the long silence.

"We have to go find him," he said quietly. "We all realize that right?"

"You are indeed right. It has to be us," Yama said.

Sparkie lifted his head up from the nearby grass where he had been eating during the silence and neighed approvingly, as if to say, I'm in, let's go.

The four new friends looked at each other and nodded silently, climbing down the wall walking into the village to begin gathering supplies for the biggest journey of their lives.

TO BE CONTINUED